Nun With a Gun
Town with No Name

Jon Gray Lang

Machines of the Infinite Press

Nun with a Gun - Town With No Name

This is a work of fiction. Names, characters, organizations, places, events and incidents are either products of the author's imagination or used fictitiously. Any resemblance to actual persons, living or dead or actual events is purely coincidental.

Copyright © 2018 Jon Gray Lang

All rights reserved.

No part of this book may be reproduced in any form or by any means without the written permission of the author, Jon Gray Lang or the publisher – Machines of the Infinite Press

Nun with a Gun - Town With No Name

To Sergio Leone, for the genre of Western you helped spawn.

Nun with a Gun - Town With No Name

Arrival

She appeared on the horizon like a mirage on a hot sunny day. She came with no horse, no wagon and no donkey. Only the two legs the Lord gave her propelled her into our little town.

She wore the colors of black and white as if they were branded into her skin. Her habit shadowed her face while her skirt billowed around her. Her bright eyes were sharp, like a hawk. Many an eye turned at her passing down the dusty street. Many an

Nun with a Gun - Town With No Name

evil man cowered under that gaze as she passed them by.

About her waist hung a gun belt. Well-worn was the leather and the steel of the Colt Peacemaker gleamed in the sun. From one wrist dangled a string of prayer beads made of darkest ebony. A single cross hung at the end and it swayed with the movement from her steps.

She read the signs emblazoned above each business on our main street as she passed them by. The Feed Store, The Bank and others were left in her wake. She came to a stop in front of the only saloon left in our dying town, The Bronze Dogie.

She pushed through the grimy saloon doors and into the darkened interior. The place reeked of tobacco smoke, sweat stained bodies and the effects of too much liquor. She peered at the bleary faces as they stared back at her. With a slow, practiced motion, she swept the road dust from her habit until it reflected in the dim lighting.

The left saloon door swayed from her passing until the hinge broke and it clattered loudly to the wooden flooring.

Town with No Name

Her eyes pierced the low light of the interior of the saloon before they settled on the man she was looking for. He stood there in his threadbare railroad man's cap while the coal dust that was embedded deeply into the folds of his skin pulled him into the shadows. His eyes grew small at her approach and he downed his shot with alacrity. As he flipped a silver dollar to the barkeep, he stepped away from the table.

Nun with a Gun - Town With No Name

But he didn't move fast enough. Before the coin finished its flashy arc, she grabbed him by his coal stained shoulder and forced him into a spin. A small cry escaped him as he fell back into the seat he had just vacated. Her dark skirts rustled in the sudden silence as she slid into the nail board bench across from him.

"Barkeep? Two whiskeys." The words fell from her lips, like nails slowly pulled from a coffin only to strike the dirt below.

As she waited for the two thumb smudged glasses to arrive, she glared at the man across from her. His corpulent belly was framed by suspenders as it protruded over the waistline of his heavily stained slacks. The two glasses hit the table with a thump and a puddle formed underneath them. Eventually the railroad man dropped his eyes and pulled another silver dollar from his well-worn pocket.

He felt her eyes on him as he nervously twirled the dirty glass between his work blackened hands. It was with an overwhelming sense of fear that he brought the glass to his lips and noisily drank it down. The glass clumped to the table.

"I didn't know, you see?" he pleaded with her. "I just brought them in and dropped them out there. I… I don't know where they are." Beads of sweat glistened on his face before he looked to the left and right. He gulped loudly. "Uh, Wallace might know. He's off at the cat-house in this here town. They don't have the prettiest doves there but uh…"

She slid the second dirty glass over to him. The sound of it grinding its way to him made him look down. A dainty finger stuck out of it. Blood slowly spiraled into the liquid from the severed digit. It was when he recognized the tattoo of a ring stamped into the finger that his eyes grew wide.

Suddenly, she grabbed him by the front of his ragged shirt and picked up the glass. She forced the glass into his mouth and waited until it was emptied, finger and all. Tears coursed down his cheeks as he choked on the woman's finger. His struggles grew more insistent before her fist came up and knocked him out of the chair and his body slammed into the wall.

She rose with a flourish and a single beam of light flashed across her face. The cross that dangled from her fist winked in the sudden brightness. The Lord's will burned in her eyes. The other patrons cowered away from her as her heels clicked into the rotting wood of the floor on her way out.

The bartender waved over a young boy who sat beside the piano. He scrawled something onto a napkin and shoved it into the lad's hands along with a couple of nickels. "Take this over to the Melendez twins. Now!" The boy was sent reeling toward the door and fell through to the porch outside. As he picked himself up, he saw her stalk toward the little town's house of ill repute.

Nun with a Gun - Town With No Name

Shadow

With the hastily scrawled note clutched tightly in his hand, the boy kept his eyes glued to the back of the mysterious woman in black. Everything about her screamed danger but at the same time, he felt he had little to fear from her. She had a presence about her that no man or woman he had ever met matched. Even the nuns he had seen were as unlike her as she was to everyone else.

Nun with a Gun - Town With No Name

He continued to follow her as she moved silently toward the Bella's Cage. She kept to the shadows and her movements were fluid, like a snake. Once she was closer to the bordello, she slowed down. She leaned against a post and put something in her mouth while she kept an eye on the front door. A glint sparkled in her eyes as she watched a couple of the townsmen entered the establishment.

The boy's foot squelched in the mud and she spun around with her pistol in hand. An unlit match dangled from her lips while her eyes searched him as a hawk does prey. He felt like a tiny mouse under her gaze and he froze. The match hung like an unspoken promise in the light of the bright sun.

Her voice crossed the distance but it felt like a whisper against his cheek, "Why are you following me little man?"

In sudden fear, he broke off the chase and ran as fast as he could to the back entrance of the Bella's Cage. She threw a half smile to his back before she holstered her gun and made her way to the front entrance.

    The child glanced over his shoulder to see if she followed but she was gone.

Nun with a Gun - Town With No Name

Snake Eyes

He stepped into one of the back rooms of Bella's Cage and found Tuco at cards. He marveled at the snake tattoo that crawled down the man's left arm. The scales glistened in the afternoon light while the eyes on his fist seemed to watch him.

Three other men were with Tuco at the gambling table. It took a moment but the boy recognized two of them as having arrived in town with the twins. The other wasn't a man he'd seen

Nun with a Gun - Town With No Name

before but he had the dead eyes of a gambler.

Hesitantly, he tapped Tuco's shoulder and proffered the note. Tuco eyed the kid and then tore the note from his hand. He quickly read through it before he growled and passed it on to one his men.

"Well aint that the most unlikely thing I've ever heard. Some nun is causing a ruckus?" uttered one of the rough and tumbles at the table.

Tuco turned to the boy, "She look like trouble?"

The boy stopped and thought a moment. He shook his head but then suddenly nodded.

"A nun up here?" cried the other man. "And she beat that hoghead down in a flat second?"

The gambler's eyes brightened at the query, "A nun you say? Is she tall for a woman? Black hair and eyes like the devil?" After a nod from boy, he rambled, "I've heard a few stories about a traveling nun. Dangerous with a pistol and a fist."

Nun with a Gun - Town With No Name

Tuco eyed the man. "Spit it out sharper. We aint got all day."

"Well, the stories I've heard is she used to travel with one of them Wild West shows back East. She was billed as a Trick shooter but the big rumor was she got hired on as a boxer. She would fight anyone. Men, women, it didn't matter. Hell in some of them tales I've heard, she even fought a bear!"

The piano in the main room could no longer be heard. What sounded like shouting took its place through the slim walls.

The gambler leaned into the table with a conspiratorial wink, "Something happened to her and she left to find God. Or God found her more like. She's a special one alright. Some say she can read your sins in your eyes and mete out the punishment to match it."

He leaned back and an ace slipped out of his sleeve to fall to the floor below, "The sisters took her in and now they send her out. From what I've heard, they call her, God's Judgment."

Nun with a Gun - Town With No Name

Tuco kicked the table into the gambler and yanked his pistol clear of its holster. Two shots were fired and the man slumped to the floor. A handful of aces fell out of his coat.

"The Melendez boys don't tolerate no cheatin'!"

Just then, shots rang out from the main room.

Bullets & Brouhaha

The front room stank of death and powder. Blood was sprayed on the painted walls and two corpses lay crumpled on the floor. One was sprawled under a table in a pile of splintered wood while the other was slumped around the corner of the bar. A thin trail of blood formed a puddle between them.

Tuco's boots splashed through the puddle when he flipped over the body under the table. His boot prints traced a path behind him as he walked over to the remains of the other one.

The young boy stole a glance at the body behind the bar. A glistening snake ran down the man's right arm, its scales as still as the dead.

A cry of anguish escaped Tuco before he cursed loudly and cried, "Who did this?"

The only reply was the stampede of the boots on the wooden floor of those left standing and the squeak of the hinges on the swinging door as they bolted for the outside.

He grabbed one of the working women as she tried to get past him, "Who killed my brother?"

She whimpered as the sound of a hammer being pulled back on a pistol echoed in the room. "Tell me who did this."

A voice that lacked all emotion cut through the silence, "Stop."

Nun with a Gun - Town With No Name

Corsets & Curiosity

A girl, not much older than the boy, appeared at the top of the roughshod staircase. The lace of her blouse fluttered as her pointing finger dropped to her side. The boy was entranced at the sight of her. He didn't know this young girl. He hadn't seen her about town before.

She was followed by an older woman whose attractiveness had been marred. The long scar that ran from chin to cheek rippled as anger twisted her face. She was as quiet as the graveyard when her fingers moved in quick succession to the young lady.

The little girl nodded before that same dead voice crawled out from her throat, "Let her go."

Tuco cursed again and pushed the woman he held against him away. Her arms searched for purchase as she crashed into the table and fell heavily to the floor.

"You again?" Tuco brandished his pistol in their direction. "I thought Cavanaugh had run you out of town."

The clicks of hammers being pulled back resounded around the main room. The two ruffians grabbed at their gun belts but slowly pulled their hands away as every single one of the ladies of the bordello had a pistol aimed in their direction. A rough laugh tore loose from Tuco as he mimed shooting the woman known as the Silent Madam.

They say she'd been a prostitute for most of her life and she had been a pretty one. As the story goes, in a fit of rage she had cursed a shiftless brigand. In reply, he had cut her tongue from her mouth then scarred her pretty face for life. Soon after she had disappeared, that man had died.

Tuco laughed again as he de-cocked his Dragoon revolver and slipped it back into its holster. "You tell me what happened here, Scarface, and I won't come back to burn you out."

The Silent Madam and the young girl who was her mouthpiece slowly came down the stairs. The flick of her fan being opened cracked across the room like a whip.

"The madam bids me to tell you that a sister of the order came here. She and your brother had words," a chilling smile split the girls face, "And she won that argument."

Tuco grunted as he hooked his thumbs into his belt. "What do you reckon they had words on?"

The fingers of the madam flew rapidly through a series of patterns. "It had something to do with a wagonload of stolen

Chinese women."

Tuco's eyes tightened at the word Chinese. "Enough. Keep your women silent or this place will be known as the house of tongue-less whores." He motioned to his two men and they stepped outside.

"Cavanaugh needs to hear this."

Dead Silence

Small gauge rail tracks could be seen far to the South by the woman in black. The rope in her hand went slack and she pushed the wounded man forward, "No rest until we get there."

He turned to her with anger in his eyes but the Peacemaker in her hand glinted with promise. Corporal Wallace spit into the dirt before he continued to lead the way. The sun beat mercilessly on their skulls as they continued to walk through the wind swept

Nun with a Gun - Town With No Name

countryside.

He stumbled and sagged onto the dusty ground. Things had not gone in his favor since the end of the war. Bad choices had led him to running with Major Cavanaugh's gang and bad choices were all he had left. A small part of him was sickened by what they had planned for those foreign women but a man had to survive; a man had to eat.

Then this banshee had shown up out of nowhere with his name on her lips. And as soon as the word Chinese had rolled out of her mouth, his hands had begun to sweat. Henry had charged her but she had knocked him into a table with one hit. When Paco had yanked out his gun, Wallace had pulled his Griswold free. But it slipped loose from his fingers. Before he even knew it, he had been shot in the gut and both Henry and Paco were dead.

The Corporal was in sad shape. His blood soaked the front of his shirt down into his pant leg. He reached to press on his hole in his gut but the rope around his wrists kept his hands away. She yanked on the rope and he falteringly stood back up. On wobbly legs, he continued onward.

"Water…" asked the Corporal. "Please sister, some water."

"When we get there," she answered. "How much further?"

He looked up from his boots and searched the horizon westward. Something glimmered in the sun, "almost there." His pace quickened.

As Wallace staggered along, she was just able to make out a few open top wagons with a rusted water buffalo coupled together. Two of the wagons lay on their side with the shattered spindles of the wheels sticking up like broken grave markers.

The Corporal slumped against the water buffalo and twisted the spigot but it was dry. It had been shot up a while ago and the ground underneath had soaked up all the water that had once resided in it. Dejectedly he fell to the ground and gasped, "Water… please."

The nun ignored him as she inspected the broken wagons.

Nun with a Gun - Town With No Name

Bullet holes had splintered the wood and torn some of the wheels apart. A handful of dead men lay amongst the wreckage, their bodies riddled with holes. The only sign left were the wagon tracks that moved off to the North.

When she came back to the water buffalo, Corporal Wallace lay dead.

Nun with a Gun - Town With No Name

House of the Dead

Tuco dismounted and tied up the stallion to the large statue of the brass bull which dominated the courtyard. A low chuckle escaped as he appraised it. Apparently the family that used to own the property prized themselves on the beef they raised. Never mind that the previous owners now only occupied the recently dug holes in the back acreage.

Tuco spit a wad of tobacco at the beast before he turned for the house.

He stepped in slowly through the front doors of the old Spanish villa. Some of the original opulence still hung in places but dirt had piled up in the corners. It still carried that abandoned feeling. Even though the Major had come to call it home as of late.

He heard Cavanaugh rummaging around and found him in the back study. He stood there with a fistful of papers while the blast streaked safe hung open.

"Major?"

Cavanaugh turned and eyed Tuco. He set the papers down on the partially burnt desk. "What are you doing here? Shouldn't you be at the Dogie keeping an eye out?"

Tuco grabbed a tumbler and poured himself a shot of whiskey. "That's why I'm here chief. There's been trouble in town and I figured I'd be the one to tell you."

"Have a drink, why don't you," grunted Cavanaugh. "Trouble eh? Those China shave tails been raising a fair fuss out here too.

Tuco muttered, "You still got 'em here?"

"Takes the Doc a while to break a girl into a proper shake." The Major poured himself a slug, "Anyway, I've been waiting on a better payout from Crawford at the miner's camp. Their last three were given the rice bowl and candle." With a wink he said, "He's getting pretty desperate."

Tuco's laugh was a rough and ugly thing. He'd seen that trick before. Once a China girl was worn out, she was locked in a cage with a rice bowl and candle. They only had three options once that candle went out. They were expected to starve to death or take their own lives. Sometimes you had to do the work yourself and leave what's left of them in a shallow grave.

"Well boss," Tuco growled. "Some catholic sister's been causing trouble in town. Wallace has gone missing. The train man is dead and so is Beekman." He slammed the glass against the desk, "And so is my brother."

Nun with a Gun - Town With No Name

Cavanaugh's eyes perked at the word sister. "The nun alone?"

"Don't know boss but I'm going to kill her. And I'm going to make it slow."

Clothed in Dirt

Crusty dried earth reached skyward like recent mudflows from the ruts left by many a wagon wheel. Though the tracks led down into a small valley, the nun had chosen to climb upwards. She slithered her way amongst the greenery that grew sparsely along the tops of the valley walls until she found a decent vantage point over what was little more than an occupied gulch.

A decrepit Spanish villa with a sagging roof and broken tiles about its cracked walls sat forlornly in the middle of the open land. The trail that she had been following was cut though by a tiny creek before it entered the valley. She brought the spyglass that she had taken from the dead corporal back to the villa but there was little to be seen until a horse was brought out into the courtyard. She watched as a doppelganger of the big Californian she had shot in the brothel rode back in the direction of town.

The villa remained undisturbed for some time until the serenity was interrupted by a couple of wagons being hitched up to horses behind the home. Both wagon beds were topped by an iron cage. She watched as canvas covers were pulled over the top and secured along the sides while rust rained down upon the dirt below. But it was the line of women chained together in their tattered silk finery that caught her eye.

She focused the spyglass on them as they were unchained and then led into the wagons only to have the cage doors locked behind them. The first wagon was loaded with eight of the captive women and a growl escaped her as the last seven were being loaded into the next wagon. The young girl at the end made a break for it once the chains were off. The sound of the shot echoed in the little canyon long after the girl fell to the ground and lay there unmoving.

Once the door on the second wagon had been locked, two men dragged her body over to the small family cemetery where a collection of mounds that barely looked a month old dominated the site. Her body was unceremoniously thrown onto a pile of refuse where bits of multi-colored silk fluttered in the dry wind.

The snap of a whip echoed up from the ranch and the wagons rolled past the walls of the villa. The horses followed the road that led to the very canyon edge that the sister watched from. A grim smile lit up her face.

Nun with a Gun - Town With No Name

Bridled Anger

Tuco threw the reins of his horse to one of his underlings as he dismounted quickly. The streets of the town were mostly empty and he preferred it that way. It was easier to keep people out of the way or to trap them if needed.

"You find her?" he asked of the man who tied the reins around the post.

The man gulped loudly, "No Tuco. We aint found her

nowheres."

Tuco grabbed him by the front of his shirt, "Nothing? Didn't find a damn thing?" The ugly little brute's feet kicked wildly as he was lifted off the ground, "You sure you were looking?"

"Yes sir, Tuco sir." He began to sweat profusely, "I swears we did but she aint here and no one done seen her leave. Last we heard is she took Wallace out of Bella's and disappeared." He whispered conspiratorially, "Maybe that cut madam knows a thing or two…"

Tuco dropped him. A look of pure disgust lit up his eyes as Tuco dusted off his shoulders, "Make sure my horse is watered."

He turned around and walked over to the Cage and his hands curled into fists.

Shod in Metal

She could hear the wheels bouncing on the trail and the quick clops of the horses as they came closer. The splash of it cutting through the creek echoed off the narrow canyon walls. Her eyes grew wide in anticipation and she could almost smell the sweat in the air.

The wagon came rolling around the corner and she heard the shout of "Whoa!" as the wet wheels slid on the dirt. She stepped to the right as the wagons narrowly missed her and came to a stop.

"Damn fool woman!" cried the driver of the first wagon. "Why are you out in the road?"

Just over his shoulder, she could see the frightened faces of the China girls as they peered out at her. The gunman to his left brought up his shotgun but it was already too late for him. The crack of her pistol reverberated off the canyon walls and his head rocked back. The shotgun fell from his nerveless fingers. Before the driver could even shout, another shot rang out and he slipped off the bench to collapse in the road dust.

Voices rang out from the wagon in the rear but she was already in motion. She swooped down to grab the shotgun and rolled into a slide under the wagon. Her pistol cracked again and the leg of a man running toward her exploded before he flopped to the ground. Her next shot tore through his hat and buried itself in his head.

"Should be two more..." she muttered.

Nun with a Gun - Town With No Name

A man's voice shouted out, "Who's out there? What you want?"

She rolled to the other side of the wagon and brought up the shotgun. Two men still sat on the bench of the second wagon. The hammer slapped home on the shotgun and they both ducked from the pellet spray. She ran toward them and brought up her pistol. Two more shots were fired and the canyon was wracked with noise. The first one missed but the second found its mark. He toppled from the bench as the second driver brought up his gun. She was close enough now that she couldn't miss with the shotgun and it barked in her hands. The driver's face pulped under the blast and his body slumped to the side.

The shotgun dropped from her hands. She rifled through the pockets of the dead men until she found the ring of keys. It only took a moment before both cages were unlocked. She waved the women out of the wagons and waited until they had all freed themselves. Each of them stood timidly under the gaze of this giant woman in the black and white of the missionaries.

The sister's mouth felt rusty as the Mandarin words slipped past her lips, "Come with me and be free of these shackles."

Girdled in Secrets

That damned madam with the cut tongue knew he was coming, it seemed. She just stood there at the bar with that odd little girl next to her while one of her women tickled the piano keys in the background.

The smell of eggs and bacon hung thick in the air and it made him hungry. People shuffled out of his way as he moved toward her and her eyes sparkled in the morning sun like she knew his darkest thoughts.

The emotionless voice that crawled out of the little girl's throat stopped him in his tracks, "Clementine? Why don't you see what this gentleman wants…?"

Clementine made a beeline for him but he pushed her away, "I aint here to satisfy no urges woman."

The madam's lips curled into a hard smile as the little one who acted as her voice spoke out, "Urges are what we live on here. What else would someone such as you come here for?"

His hand snaked out and grabbed the young girl by the neck but he hesitated when he felt a hand on his wrist. He could feel the strength in that grip. He could feel the promise. The little girl's dead eyes bored into his and he pushed her away and spun on the madam, "I came here for answers wag-tail, not to play your little games."

Her eyes sparkled with a dark mirth as the little girl's voice drove shivers up his spine. "Answers have costs. Are you willing to pay?"

People usually stank of fear when he confronted them but this cursed nanny didn't see him as anything more than a mark. A sour grunt escaped him and the stink of it caused the madam's eyes to water. "Where'd that nun say she was goin'?"

"She didn't call out no destination," answered Clementine with a lilt to her tongue. "She just grabbed that fool Corporal. That is, after she shot up your man… and your brother…"

His face blurred into a mask of rage as he moved toward Clementine. The slow click of a hammer being pulled back behind him brought him to a standstill.

That monotone voice broke the tension. "Now, now señor Melendez. That's twice you've threatened to shoot one of my girls. I don't take kindly to that. Maybe you should be asking yourself what she wanted with Corporal Wallace. What would he know that no one else here could?"

Surprise blanked his expression for a moment and was then

replaced with a brutish grin. "Looks like I don't need you for nothing at all." A sneer lit up his eyes as he tipped his hat in the madam's direction, "Ladies."

That dead voice rant out as he made his way back to the door, "Third time's the charm, Tuco. Third time's the charm."

In a rage, he kicked the door open as that promise hung in the air.

Nun with a Gun - Town With No Name

Away From Prying Eyes

The two empty wagons waited forlornly in the rutted tracks of the trail while the hot sun blazed overhead. Sister swept at the path to the old mine with a large scrub brush branch. She kept at it until the ground looked as untrammeled as it had in ages. With a small satisfied nod, she threw the branch into the back of one of the wagons before she hopped onto the driver's bench.

In her halting Mandarin, she had struggled to convince these sing-song girls that they needed to hide. They wanted to go back to the little town but that was the most dangerous place for them to go. She couldn't leave them wandering the plains without a guide and this sister's work was far from done.

But it wasn't until she mentioned Fahn Quai that they finally listened. They followed her to the abandoned mine armed with the guns from the dead slavers. Fear was writ large on their faces before she left them but she promised she would get them back to San Francisco in safety.

With a flick of the whip, the horses leapt forward and dragged the wagons with them. Her eyes sparkled in the bright sun. The only thing left to do was to lay a false trail away from here to give her the time needed for the rest of the plan.

Nun with a Gun - Town With No Name

Trappings and Habits

On their way back out to the abandoned wagons north of the old rail tracks, Tuco and his men rode like Death himself was after them. Dust plumed upward into the wind and shifted to the East as they brought their horses to a standstill.

The desiccated corpses of the rival gang still lay scattered around the empty wagons. A grim smile lit upon Tuco's face. Those yacks had fallen like a stack of chips in a bad game of Faro and snatching those China girls had been easy work. The smile fell from Tuco's when they found Wallace's carcass keeping the water buffalo company.

It was that sonk Cole who found her dusty boot prints mixed in with the wheel ruts from their wagons. He let the fool lead the way as they followed the trail into the plains. Once they came within sight of the villa, her boot prints disappeared on the rock face. No hide nor hair of her was to be found close by.

"Boys!" Tuco shouted. "Get a wiggle on and find me that devil of a sister, now!

As his men scoured out in search of any sign of her, he kicked back and watched for anything on the horizon that caught his eye. He felt more than heard one of his men riding back.

"You find anything Boone?" Tuco grunted.

Boone wiped the dust from his face, "I found Virgil. He, Sam and a couple others are lying in the road to the mining camp. They've uh, all been shot up."

Nun with a Gun - Town With No Name

"The wagon's there too?"

Boone pulled his hat low, "Tracks stop at the bodies but then cut back."

Anger twisted at Tuco's eyes. That nun was making a habit of being in all the wrong places and leaving the dead in her wake. Just then a plume of dust far to the East caught his eye and a wolfish grin lit his face.

"Call the boy's back, Boone. We're going hunting."

Nun with a Gun - Town With No Name

Brush & Bramble

Corporal Wallace's spyglass rested against her eye as she spied on the broken down villa but the yard beyond the crumbling low wall remained still and empty. The route she had taken the wagons had been long and circuitous before she had abandoned them back a ridge or two.

The sound of a slight scuff sounded off to her right. Her eyes flicked in that direction but there was nothing to be seen but

Nun with a Gun - Town With No Name

Mormon tea and a few scrub oak that clung to the dusty soil. The rustle of a branch caught her ears before she slowly reached for her pistol but the click of a hammer from behind her made her hesitate.

Dust plumed into the air from horses ridden hard as they came to a stop in front of where she lay. She counted three men when a couple more popped up out of the weeds. The tromp of boots behind her stopped her from reaching for her gun.

She spread eagled out in the dirt as the point of a barrel pressed into the back of her skull.

"My, my. You are a strapper aint you?" rang out a man's voice tinged with a Spanish accent. "I didn't expect to find you above the bend."

Her gun was wrenched free from its holster and the clatter it made as it hit the dust put it a few feet away.

The butt of Tuco's Paterson cracked into the back of her skull, "Can't say I'm pleased."

Nun with a Gun - Town With No Name

Her eyes fluttered open as the floorboard jounced underneath her. Rusty iron bars crisscrossed her view when a vaguely familiar face took up the sky.

Cole started when he saw Tuco wrap his hands around the sister's throat inside the cage of the cat wagon. "Hey Tuco, I wouldn't do that if I were you. Pretty sure Cavanaugh's gonna want her alive."

With an unsatisfied grunt, the man's hands left her neck. The rough road underneath the moving wagon jostled her once again.

As she caught herself, she barely heard the words as his fist crashed into her chin, "After the Major's done with you; you're mine sister. You're mine."

Nun with a Gun - Town With No Name

Drawn & Cornered

The groans of a woman intermixed with the meaty thuds from fists as they slammed into flesh. Major Cavanaugh muttered under his breath as the racket resounded out into the hallway he stood in. The scratched, golden pocket watch slipped into his vest pocket as he bit down hard on the cigarillo that jutted from his mouth.

"Tell me where they are, woman!"

Nun with a Gun - Town With No Name

Tuco jumped in surprise when the door to the cellar opened. The Major stood there and looked nonplussed. His gang glanced back with guilt in their eyes. Tuco leapt out of the way as the lit cigarillo sailed toward him. This left the Major with an unobstructed view of the sister as she hung by her wrists from a rope that dangled from the rafters above.

"What did I say to you, Tuco?" The Major waited but Tuco just hid his hands and looked at the ground. "What did I say?"

"The nun was off limits," Cole piped in.

A capricious grin flitted across Cavanaugh's face, "That's right. The nun is off limits. Does she look like he understood that, Cole?"

"No sir! Not at all!"

"Thank you, Cole." Cavanaugh strolled over and glared directly into Tuco's eyes, "Now Mr. Melendez, if an idiot like Cole can grasp this, what does that say about you?" The Major's boot slammed into the big man's stomach and he sprawled out like a sick calf on the ground as he gasped for air.

"Surrounded by a bunch of dimwits," grunted Cavanaugh before he turned on his men. "Check the abandoned mine, you dolts! There aint nowhere else those two timing slummys could be. Go!"

Boone and Cole grabbed Tuco and dragged him out of the cellar.

Cavanaugh turned to the bloodied woman whose face rang with defiance, "What am I going to do with you sister? What am I going to do with you?"

Nun with a Gun - Town With No Name

Providence or Autonomy

Cavanaugh spied a crumpled slip of paper at the nun's feet. Curiosity got the better of him as he retrieved it. The woman's eyes burned as he uncrumpled the note but he laughed anyway.

"A vow of silence, eh? I can see why Tuco is so taken with you."

Slowly, he slid the note into his vest pocket as he cupped his chin in thought, "I must say this is an unprecedented opportunity!

Nun with a Gun - Town With No Name

I can't remember the time I had a member of the clergy as a captive audience. Just so we understand ourselves, there has been a part of our God given religion which has always concerned me."

He groused, "How can Man have free will when God is omnipotent?"

"Now, if God knows every single decision you're going to make in your life, then you can't change anything. Free will would just be a pipe dream." He peered into her eyes, "Do you get me?'"

Muffled shouts sounded in the distance through the cellar walls. As her mouth opened, he patted his pocket, "Vow of silence, remember?"

Cavanaugh looked up as began pacing. "If the Almighty is omnipotent, then how can any decision a man makes be considered free will?"

As gunfire filtered through the floor above the cellar his voice grew louder, "I didn't want to choose this life, but every decision I made led me down it. If God knew, in his omnipotence, that was what I would do, well then that's fate. Aint no two ways about it."

"Let's take you for instance, Sister. You've gone and murdered some of my men." His eyes lit with a craftiness, "And I can guarantee they weren't the first ones you've ever ended. You made the choice to break that Commandment, in the name of the church, to boot! And the Man Above knows you made those choices. Just as he knew them before you existed. Hell, probably at the beginning of time itself."

"You're a killer just like me, Sister. Born to be one, bred to be one and fated to be one. And you never had a real choice in the matter. Not one."

Nun with a Gun - Town With No Name

Ash and Cracklings

The last words she heard from the Major rang in her ears, "I seem to recall a story about a young girl who was born again, from the ashes of her life. I figure, she'd be about your age. Have you heard this one? No?" His teeth had glinted in the lamplight as the echo of gunfire grew louder.

"Now, from what I remember, and my memory aint what it used to be, this little lass escaped from her home as it burned to the ground. The bodies of her family, murdered before her innocent eyes, were quickly consumed by the flames as the roof beams crashed down upon their blackened bones."

His grim smile had sent her mind reeling and his words continued, "Now as I was saying, this callow lady escaped with her life while the stink of her parent's roasting flesh billowed around her. But she didn't leave empty handed. Oh no. From what I hear, she left with her father's pistol and it was still hot from the fire. Stories say that the cross in the grip burned its way into her left palm and she didn't even notice."

Her hand had closed reflexively as she tried to look away.

But still his voice droned on, "She went on and took down the entire gang that was responsible. Murdered every single one of the bastards, this little girl did. One hell of a killing spree and rightfully so. But here's where the story gets strange."

His eyes lit into her soul, "Seemed she had a taste for the violence, for the death. She went after anyone on a poster and everyone of 'em came back dead. It got so bad that she ended up on one of them posters herself."

The spark of a match being lit made her flinch. As he blew it out, he had smiled at her reaction. "She disappeared for a while before she was seen again at a Wild West show." Dark mischief curdled the words, "You sure you've never heard this tale before?"

But she knew this story well… too well. Her memories invaded her mind and dragged her kicking and screaming back into them and wouldn't let her pull free. She was lost in the past as she stumbled away from the burning building Tuco had caged her in.

The heat of the flames licking its sides warmed the sands under her bare feet.

Nun with a Gun - Town With No Name

Up Stakes

Before the Major had run up the rickety steps to cellar, Doctor Villega had come in to keep an eye on that devil of a woman. Tricky as she was, even she wouldn't be able to escape in her present condition.

A quick laugh escaped him as he thought back on the expression left on her face. He had torn her world asunder and she hadn't expected it. Funnily enough, he had expected more from her. It was rare to meet a legend and a boogeyman to boot. Rare indeed.

As Cavanaugh stepped out of the barn, he ducked as a bullet pinged the stucco right next to his head. Madness had sprung like wildfire over the plains surrounding his villa. Gunfire exploded into the night sky while bottles of flames burst against the sides of the buildings of his hideout. His plans had gone awry.

His men looked away as he marched his way through them to see what the commotion was.

"Damn fool miners," he cursed loudly. "Came to take what they think is theirs and that witch of a nun stole them from me!"

Cavanaugh pulled the trigger on his pistol and watched as one of the miners dropped to the ground. That broke them. They ran off into the desert night and left him nothing in return.

The heat of the villa as it burned to the ground radiated against his back, "Curse that woman. Cole you go check on Doc, will ya?"

His man slipped into the darkness but was occasionally lit by the light of the flames as he made his way back to the cellar. Tuco stepped out of the darkness and stopped in front of him.

"How many got away, Melendez?" the Major groused.

Tuco pulled his hat off and wiped at the ash that collected on the brim, "Not enough to sell them China girls to. The days of that hole in the ground are done."

Cavanaugh spun as Cole's hand gripped his shoulder. The fool stumbled back at the grim visage on the Major's face.

Cole stuttered out as he held his hands in front of him, "Villega is dead, sir. And I aint seen no sign of the Sister."

Cavanaugh didn't make a sound but the men nearest him stepped back.

Boone's voice came like a whisper out of the night, "Sir? What should we do with the bodies?"

"Leave them for the crows. We've got work to do."

Blood and Darkness

As the fiery light behind her faded, the nun slowly came back to herself. Her ribs hurt and her wrists burned. Dried blood coated the skin across her split open knuckles.

When each step moved her further away from the villa, the labored breathing of someone behind her sounded out. She spun quickly, but the night sky was dark without the presence of the moon. Only the pinpricks of the stars lit the way.

Nun with a Gun - Town With No Name

She stopped for a moment until a slight feminine form walked into her. She caught her as she slipped in the sand. A small cry in Mandarin escaped the mystery woman's mouth.

"Who are you?" The sister whispered harshly into the darkness. As her hands helped slide the small lady to the ground, she caught one of the woman's hands in her own. Something felt strange about it, but she kept her mind on keeping the girl from falling.

As the woman slumped into a seated position, it finally struck her. There were only nine fingers.

The crunch of steel shod wheels cutting their way through the crust of the earth caught her ears as the light of two handheld lanterns crested the hill they lay on top of. With the last of her energy, she prepared for a fight she didn't think she could win.

But she relaxed when the lanterns lit up the face of the young boy from town and the strange girl who lived in the brothel. She watched as the two children stopped the wagon and came over to help her lift the tiny Chinese woman into the back of the wagon. They helped her up as she pulled herself up.

The wagon trundled back the way it came and the Sister stared at the face of the woman in the wagon with her. She suddenly remembered, "I know you. You knocked that sawbones out. You carried me away from there until I could stand on my own again. I owe you my life."

The Chinese woman's eyes remained closed as her breathing leveled out. The nun relaxed and let the weight of the world fall from her shoulders and her eyes quickly fluttered shut.

Nun with a Gun - Town With No Name

Tunnel Vision

She woke from a low slung bed with a great indrawn breath. The stink of old straw permeated the air as her eyes tracked wildly around the room she found herself in. Slowly, she settled on the face of the Chinese woman, O-Lan, the one who had escaped with her.

O-Lan's cuts had been cleaned and she looked at peace. The sister looked down at her own hands and cloth bandages encircled her wrists. She felt along her head and another bandage was wrapped tightly across her forehead.

With some effort, she slowly lifted herself to a sitting position to see more of the room. Beds were lined up in rows against the stone back walls and across from each other in what she could only assume was a wine cellar.

Many of the beds were occupied by the young women she had last seen in the mines. A sense of accomplishment settled into her bones. She was startled when she felt a hand touch her on the shoulder.

"Would you like some water, sister?" asked the young girl from the wagon.

A simple smile painted her lips, "Coffee. Black if you've got it."

The madam appeared behind the girl and spoke quickly with her fingers. The adolescent girl nodded and moved off toward the single staircase. The sister watched until she disappeared around the corner.

The madam smiled politely before taking a seat next to the sister. Her hands spoke quickly, "We got your message as you can see. None of them are badly hurt. Even you and the one you came in with only suffered some cuts and bruises."

After a moment, the nun signed back, "How are things out there? Is it bad?"

The madam shook her head in the negative. She leveled a frank gaze at the sister, "How did you know I would help them? How did you know I would help you?"

The nun leaned in and gave the madam a long appraising look before she shifted back. Her fingers moved in quick succession, "I've heard stories of a Pinkerton woman who disappeared into the West. From those tales, I hear she works tirelessly to end the slave trade of girls and women to the brothels of mining camps and small towns."

A shy grin colored her face, "These stories are quite popular amongst the sisters of my order. We strive to end this devilish trade as well, and it is good to know that we are not alone."

The madam stared at her quizzically, "But why would you think that I am this Pinkerton?"

The sister's voice echoed loudly in the cellar as she made a knifelike gesture against her face, "All of the stories talk of this woman as having a cut across her face, but she refuses to keep quiet. Even Fahn Quai herself has told me of you."

Many voices took this up and the cellar reverberated with her name, "Fahn Quai? Fahn Quai?"

O-Lan appeared behind the nun and rested her nine fingered hand against her shoulder. She waved the other girls quiet as she squeezed the shoulder tightly, "You can get us to her?"

The sister placed her hand over O-Lan's. "We can get you to her and back to your homes. It will take some time…"

O-Lan interrupted her, "We cannot go back home! Our families sold us into this servitude! We… we have nowhere else to go."

The madam reached out and covered both their hands with hers. Her fingers flew in quick succession and while everyone watched in silence, the nun translated into Mandarin, "Fahn Quai is a friend. She has helped many like you. She will know what to do."

The tension in the cellar relaxed while some of the girls translated the Mandarin into Cantonese for the other girls.

While the conversation continued, the young lady made her way down the stairs and placed a cup of hot black coffee in the sister's lap.

The monotone voice of the girl boomed loudly in the room, "The Major and his men are riding for the town. I think they mean to find you and murder you, sister. If they come across these Celestials, that little town will be filled with nothing but death."

Light of Truth

The madam's hand slipped into her lap as she stood up. Her fingers quickly signed, "Thank you, daughter."

The nun barely caught this exchange. She busily relayed the message to the rest of the women in the cellar in Mandarin. Cries of anguish filled the room when the sister felt a tug from the madam.

The madam quickly signed, "I must get my house in order

and get my girls ready."

"Do you plan to fight?" asked the sister in return.

A sad smile graced the scarred lips of the woman, "Of course. If I do not, who will?" She kissed the hand of the sister and made her way up the stairs. Her daughter followed quickly behind.

O-Lan watched this quietly before she asked, "Where does she go?"

"She goes to fight them," the nun answered. She stood up slowly and adjusted her skirts, "As do I."

The other women quieted down at this exchange. After a moment, many of them moved back to their beds. They picked up the weapons they had kept with them since they had been freed.

The sister turned to all of them, "You don't have to do this. You didn't choose to fight this battle."

O-Lan replied angrily, "We didn't choose the life that was forced on us, but we can choose to do this." She moved quickly

Nun with a Gun - Town With No Name

toward the stairs, "Are you coming?"

Nun with a Gun - Town With No Name

Leather & Tobacco

Cavanaugh's men rode hard and fast to the small town on the horizon. Their rage was palpable as they beat their foam slathered horses ever closer.

Once they crested the hill, a man seated on his horse stood starkly out against the horizon. Cavanaugh called a halt. As the rising dust plumed outward, the Major cantered over to his tracker, "what's the news, Boone?"

Nun with a Gun - Town With No Name

"Most of the townsfolk have holed up in their homes or headed out of town," he answered. "I think they can smell the trouble that's been brewin'."

The Major's face twisted into an ugly mask, "What about that witch of a sister?"

Boone gulped and his horse shied back a step, "The nun is down there, sir. I've seen her with my own eyes."

The tracker proffered the spyglass and Cavanaugh snatched it from his hands. While he scanned the streets of the town, Cole drank loudly from his canteen. Tuco lit up a cigar while Frank and Holt chewed on the jerky that they had salvaged from the villa. The other men waited on their commander.

"How many are down there?" asked the Major.

Boone sat quietly on his horse as he calculated in his head, "Besides the nun? Nine of them calico queens."

Cavanaugh stiffened and leaned forward, "I see one of our China girls down there."

Nun with a Gun - Town With No Name

"Well, there was fifteen of them, last we saw." Boone started counting on his fingers, "I'd give a guess at twenty five, then." He looked over what was left of the gang, "Only thirteen of us. We are sorely outnumbered, sir."

The clap of the spyglass being closed snapped his men out of their reverie. Cavanaugh turned to face his posse, "How about it, boys? We got twenty five fillies down there and only one of them can shoot."

Tuco growled, "That nun aint no woman. She's a curse."

"Best way to end a curse is to end it, hombre," Cavanaugh shot back. "Let's clip the horns on those painted cats! Hyaah!"

The Major shot forward and his men followed close behind. To some it seemed as if Sam Hill rode with them. To others, they were the devils and the desire for vengeance was thick.

Nun with a Gun - Town With No Name

Whisper of Silk

As the men on horses thundered closer, Ling Moy thought back on what the giant woman had said, "It's going to be loud. It's going to be frightening and you may think you're ready. But I can tell you, you're not."

Hai Tang had protested loudly at this point and Ghee Moon had laughed. The lady, all dressed in black, waited until they quieted down. "Some of you may have never shot a gun before and you're afraid you'll miss, but if you're close enough and you all fire at the same time, you'll hit something. That's the most we can hope for right now."

Ling Moy closed her eyes as the dust from the horses rose into a cloud and the pounding sound receded away from them. Her eyes opened and she peeked around the corner of the building. She watched as the horses slowed down in the middle of this dirty little town.

"Go!" O-Lan cried.

She and her fellow Chinese ran out in the street and formed a rough line behind the horsemen. They were now less than a stone's throw away from the men who had locked them up. She could hear the other girls counting slowly when a shot rang out from Hai Tang's rifle.

She cursed as those bastards turned their horses around. She pulled the hammers back on her shotgun and let loose with both barrels after the order for "Fire!" was shouted.

Nun with a Gun - Town With No Name

Adrenaline ran through her and her hands shook. She almost dropped her gun at the kick and from explosion of sound they had made. The screams of horses and men flooded out from the smoke of gunpowder.

O-Lan screamed, "Run!"

Ling Moy almost missed the command, though once it registered, she ran back into the small alley she had been waiting in. Gun fire erupted behind her and she heard screams from a couple girls, but she didn't look back.

Nun with a Gun - Town With No Name

The Hustle of Bustles

As the rifle blasts erupted into Cavanaugh's men, the sister watched as one horse fell squealing on its side, trapping its rider. Two men toppled off their horses and a third ran toward the saloon.

This horse's rider roared like a banshee as he flung burning bottles of kerosene against the sides of the saloon and it quickly caught fire. The other riders turned to give chase to the China girls.

"Now!" shouted the nun as she ran out into the street.

Gunfire burst from the high windows of the brothel and the bank. The sister stood in the middle of the street and raised her pistol to shoot one of the men as he wheeled his horse back around. He went down as a hole sprouted in his chest. The bottle of kerosene in his hand shattered against the hard ground. Flames leapt out and caught on the man trapped under his horse.

The sister ran across the street and a shot blasted into the post nearest her head. As she turned to see who fired it, a man slumped forward on his horse and the horse bolted. The nun took aim and the pistol kicked in her hands.

Cole, who had been riding next to Tuco, went down. Tuco wheeled his horse around and watched the sister run down the street into the brothel.

Nun with a Gun - Town With No Name

Trapped

Ling Moy could hear the horses behind her as she ran. She had dropped her shotgun somewhere behind her, but she had pulled the trigger twice. Its barrels were as empty as her stomach. She came back out to the main street and bullets were flying in all directions.

"Stop running you flash-girl!" roared a voice behind her.

The wooden flooring she ran across exploded and wood

fragments flew around her face. She tripped and fell into the street. The ground thumped beneath her as the horse moved closer to her. She rolled over and found herself lying in front of O-Lan. The man on the horse laughed as he aimed his pistol at them. She threw her arms over her face.

The gun in O-Lan's hands barked and the horse threw itself upward. The rider slipped off the back and tumbled to the ground. O-Lan strode forward with no fear showing on her face as she pulled the trigger on her pistol two more times.

Though muffled, Ling Moy heard O-Lan curse, "Stupid, color-seeking wolf."

Ling Moy slowly sat up when a pistol clattered next to her.

O-Lan shouted, "Get up lazy bug! We aren't done yet."

Nun with a Gun - Town With No Name

Fisticuffs

Tuco, followed quickly by two of his men, burst into the Bella's Cage. The nun stood across from them, her pistol in hand.

"Burn it!" cried Tuco.

Tuco's men threw their lit bottles of kerosene against the walls of the building. Before the bottles left their hands, the sister had pulled the trigger twice and one of the men spun as he crashed into a table. The other gang member had enough time to raise his gun before his legs were shot out beneath him. Her third shot went through the brigand's head.

Tuco raised his Paterson and squeezed the trigger but the sister had already moved. She came to a stop and they stood facing each other. Both of them pulled their triggers.

As each pistol hit a spent chamber, Tuco dropped his gun. He winked at her, "Your move, sister."

The nun flung her pistol to the side and took a boxer's stance. A smirk split its way across her face, "I'm not hanging from the rafters this time. Think you can take me, Tuco?"

A vicious grin lit up his face, "I told him I'd kill you."

With a scream he launched himself at the woman. She threw up a block against his clumsy strike and drove a fist into his sternum. His breath caught quickly as he stumbled back. She slammed another fist high into his ribs close to the armpit. He tried to pull back but she rode him up against a table. As he slipped, she step inside his defense and threw a jab under his rib cage, followed by another into the sternum.

He twisted to get away from her, but in doing so, dropped the arm protecting his face. She followed him with a quick inner shift and her fist smashed into the bottom of his jaw. He flailed wildly and she struck him repeatedly high in the ribs near the armpit. As he spun away, she drove her fists into his kidneys repeatedly.

His hand caught a chair and he was able to right himself. He threw a sloppy punch that caught a glancing blow to her temple. As she stepped back, he threw another punch but she caught his wrist. Using the momentum of his attack, she spun him and smashed his wrist into the edge of the table.

The crack of the break was loud in the confines of the room. His scream tore out and he fell to one knee. Her eyes lit up as she twisted his broken wrist and struck him repeatedly in the temple until he went limp. She kicked him square in the chest after he fell heavily to the floor.

Nun with a Gun - Town With No Name

The bursts of gunfire outside in the streets had slowed and she could hear shouting. Clementine stepped into the building and took in the sister standing with the big man, Tuco, lying on the floor.

"Any trouble, sister?"

The nun looked down at the man and back at Clementine, "He didn't know what he was getting into. Keep an eye on him, would you?"

Clementine bent down and retrieved a pistol that had a couple unspent rounds in it. With a practiced throw, she tossed it to the nun, "Of course. We're almost done outside."

As the nun stepped through the door back out into the street, Clementine turned to the man lying on the floor. His eyes fluttered open and he looked around.

"Where'd she go? I'm not done yet."

"You heard the madam's voice. Third time's the charm, Tuco." Clementine squeezed the trigger of her own pistol and

Nun with a Gun - Town With No Name

watched as his head bounced against the floor, "Third time's the charm…"

Nun with a Gun - Town With No Name

Boxed In

The sister stepped out onto the raised sidewalk along the main street of the little town. The air was filled with smoke from the burning buildings and the screams of wounded horses. Gunshots burst out until only the smoke and fire remained.

She turned her eyes to the middle of the street and Major Cavanaugh stood at one end while the brothel's madam slowly stepped out to face him.

Nun with a Gun - Town With No Name

The flat dead, voice of the daughter of the Pinkerton woman broke the silence, "How's your poor feet, Major?"

Cavanaugh's laugh was grating, "Funny, girl." His eyes lit on the scarred woman as she came to a stop across from him, "You taking me on, woman? I would've figured you'd have learned that lesson a long time ago."

The madam remained quiet as did her voice. She slowly pulled her pistol from its holster and checked to make sure it still had a few rounds in it.

Cavanaugh sneered, "When I'm done with you, demimonde, there won't be enough of you left to snore."

Her response was to simply slide her pistol home. Her right leg slipped behind her into a dueler's stance. Her right hand moved toward the holster she wore on her left hip as she stretched out her left arm and waved him on with her index and middle fingers.

His snarl whipped across the quiet and he reach for the butt of his pistol. Before he could even bring it to bear, the air cracked with a shot. His body was hammered back by one hit and then by another. His pistol slipped from his fingers before he slumped to his knees. His hand reached out before he fell face first into the dirt of the road.

The nun watched in surprise as the madam holstered her pistol and stepped out of the road. She felt a tug on her skirt and looked down at the adolescent whose voice held no emotion.

The young girl looked her square on when she said, "To cut a man's suspenders, a girl must be fast. Wouldn't you say, sister?"

Nun with a Gun - Town With No Name

A New Day

The boy looked at the long stretch of coffins that decorated the walls of the undertaker's shop before he turned back to the sister.

She left the little town as she had come to it. Alone, with no horse, no wagon or donkey. Only the two legs given by the Lord saw her way out.

Her habit had shadowed her face in the early morning sun

Nun with a Gun - Town With No Name

while the white edge of the coif fairly glowed with promise. Her black skirt rustled in the light breeze and the dust raised by her feet pillowed outward to be caught and thrown further away.

For a moment she stopped and watched the train on the horizon as it cut its way back to San Francisco. A light smile touched her lips. The Chinese women and the Madam's girls were making their way back to their new home. Fahn Quai would see them through as she had done for many others.

The words of Cavanaugh echoed within her; how can Man have free will with a God that is omnipotent? "How am I any different than he in your eyes?" she asked the sky.

She had kept her promise. A killer she may be, but she had done that much. Maybe that's all that was needed of her.

The dusty plains called to her and the hymn of Queen of the Waves came to her lips. It wafted back to the young boy who stayed behind.

About her waist hung a gun belt. Well-worn was the leather

and the steel of the Colt Peacemaker as it gleamed in the sun. From one wrist dangled a string of prayer beads made of darkest ebony and a single cross hung at the end which swayed with the movement from her steps.

The boy jumped when the burnt hinge to the right saloon door snapped and it clattered loudly to the wooden floor.

Made in the USA
Middletown, DE
13 December 2019